James Nisbeth and Co.

The Robins' Nest and where Do you Think they Built it? A

Truthful Tale

James Nisbeth and Co.

The Robins' Nest and where Do you Think they Built it? A Truthful Tale

ISBN/EAN: 9783337030421

Printed in Europe, USA, Canada, Australia, Japan

Cover: Foto ©Andreas Hilbeck / pixelio.de

More available books at **www.hansebooks.com**

THE

ROBINS' NEST;

AND

WHERE DO YOU THINK THEY BUILT IT?

A Truthful Tale.

BY A CLERGYMAN'S WIFE;

AUTHORESS OF

"INSTRUCTIVE THOUGHTS," (A SERIES OF MUSICAL COMPOSITIONS FOR THE
YOUNG).

"MAY-DAY IN OUR VILLAGE."

SIXTH THOUSAND.

LONDON:

JAMES NISBET & CO., 21, BERNERS STREET, OXFORD STREET.

1864

Come, children, come to God;
  Cast all your sins away;
Seek ye the Saviour's cleansing blood,
  Repent, believe, obey !

Say not, ye cannot come;
  For Jesus bled and died,
That none who ask in humble faith,
  Should ever be denied.

Say not, ye will not come,
  When God vouchsafes to call;
For fearful will their end be found,
  On whom His wrath shall fall.

Come, then, whoever will;
  Come, while 'tis called to-day;
Seek ye the Saviour's cleansing blood,
  Repent, believe, obey !

Perhaps some of my young readers may think **me** very silly, but I never see a party of boys "out on **a** nesting expedition," but **my** heart beats painfully; and **all the** talk **in the** world **about** "its **being no** harm," **will never** convince me, that anything which **gives** pain **to any of God's** creatures—small **or great—can be** free **from** "*harm*"—**if** it is not a *sin*. Surely "**He who feeds** the young ravens when they **cry**," **must look** with displeasure on a "cry" of pain from the tiniest feathered thing of His creating.

So many touching anecdotes of the affection and sagacity of these dear little warblers come crowding into my mind, that if I were to indulge myself, I could half fill this book with them; and then what would my young friends say? Perhaps some day I may write a child's volume, called "Anecdotes of Birds;" that is, supposing there is not one already written. Why, I believe "stories of canaries,"—dear, bright-eyed, cunning, teachable, loving canaries,—would make a book, a good-sized one too.

I was staying with a friend once, who had one of these golden pets, **which** seemed to have taken a sin-

gular dislike to the morning reading and family prayers.
The moment he saw the blessed Bible placed on the
table, though he was quiet enough before, perhaps
feeding—(for if the truth must be told, he was a bit **of**
a greedy-greedy)—perhaps sharpening his fine beak
against the lump sugar—no matter—that moment he
would "set up" singing at the top of his voice, to such
a pitch, that the wonder was the exquisite machinery
of his little throat never split, **and so have** spoilt all
his melody for ever.

Of course my friend tried to teach him better manners; and before he began to read, a handkerchief was
thrown over his cage. But Master Dick had no idea
of being silenced without rhyme or reason, as no **doubt**
he considered it; so down the saucy fellow would **hop,**
and if there was the least space uncovered, through
that loop-hole he would pop his bright-eyed head, which
he would turn knowingly on one side, and begin
chirping like a crazy bird—as much as to say, "I am
not going to be made hold my tongue, so you needn't
try."

At other times, when there was a loop-hole for him,

he would set to, and peck—peck—peck—till he got his beak through, and then did he not get angry? I need not tell you that when this part of his mischief was accomplished, he was not long in getting his pert, but handsome head through, and then began the clapper!

I seem to have a dim recollection that a cat caught this darling bird, as he was hopping about the carpet, pecking up the crumbs, so happy and so fearlessly! I don't think I love cats so well as I do dogs, on that account; though I know they are very useful, when people are "over-run with mice."

If any of you have a pet canary, or a pet bulfinch, or a tame magpie, my young friends, *never* trust your cat. Some people will say, when warned on this point, "O, but *my* cat never touches the bird, and would not hurt it if she had the opportunity." All nonsense! Cats are natural enemies to birds; and because she never *has* "touched your pet," it is no reason at all why she never *should*. Just the contrary. So take care of your favourites, dear children, and never trust stealthy, sly, bird-fancying pussy further than you can see her. Do not beat, or illtreat her, though. Recollect it is her nature to prey on birds, and as *you* must have *your* nature changed, before you can " do always that which is good," so must your poor cat, ere she leaves off to catch and eat up birds and canaries.

But, dear me, I am wandering away from the history of a pair of robins, which I hope to make very interesting to my juvenile friends ; so, without further delay, I will begin in those magic words, which have, from time out of date, caused many a gentle heart to go "pit-a-pat," and many a warm imagination to take flight into unheard-of regions, " *Once upon a time.*"

CHAPTER II.

ONCE upon a time, many years ago, before any of you, my dear young readers, had seen the glad sunshine, and the bright green fields, a little Robin Redbreast threw off his shell, and crept feebly out of his odd little cradle.

Like poor new babies, when first born, the newly-liberated prisoner, Robin, required a great deal of care and feeding from his watchful mother; for he seemed inclined to be weakly at first; but as he grew older, he began to show symptoms of great personal beauty; his breast was such a magnificent colour, something between a deep gold and a rich crimson; his eye so dark and brightsome! his feathers so soft, and brown! his feet and tail so dainty, that all the bird-gossips about the neighbourhood prophesied that he would be the handsomest redbreast that ever was seen.

Some went so far as to say he was "too beautiful to

live." This, however, was great nonsense; for I never heard of birds, nor people either, dying of beauty, any more than I have of their dying of goodness. When ignorant people say of a tolerably decent behaved baby, "Ah! bless his, or her little heart, she's too good to live," I feel inclined to say, "*Nonsense! Nonsense!*"

But to return to Master Redbreast. I give him this title, because he was the "son and heir" to all he could catch; for he was not born with a title, neither with a fortune; he had to win his bread, that is, to keep a sharp look out for every meal, and a good thing too. Lazy birds, like lazy people, are odious creatures.

Well! as this highly-favoured redbreast was one day tripping, with light step, over the fields, and turning his head from side to side, with a trifle of a consequential air, just as you see some pert young gentlemen do at times, I can fancy that many a feathered belle admiringly turned her eye upon him, and longed for Valentine's day.

Miss Jenny Wren, standing on tip-toe to gaze after him, exclaimed, with a sigh—when she thought "what a bit of a thing" she was beside him—"what a lovely fellow!" Miss Water Wagtail would pause, as she sailed gracefully over the low grass, trailing her sleek tail after her, just like a duchess's train—"Really he's not a bad looking creature, that Master Redbreast, only he thinks a little too much of his beautiful **breast** and bright eyes." While many an impudent cock-sparrow, envious of his gay colours, would sneer **and** chirp out of spite; and even the tuneful thrush, and melodious blackbird, would whisper to each other, with a self-satisfied, confidential turn of the head, " What's the use of all his good looks and fine figure, when he can't sing a note; every bird knows that beauty is only skin deep."

Master Redbreast, however, took no notice of **any of** these speeches, whether kind or unkind ; he went hopping about, picking up the tiny grubs, and, as I before said, turning his handsome head from side to side, as if he were looking for something he had not yet discovered.

Now, **I** doubt not, but being a very social bird, he felt lonely; **he** was tired of having no one to trill his morning and evening song to ; no one to care for, and call his own; no one to comfort him, when he was tired of hopping about, looking for his supper; but, above all, no one to help him build the nest he was anxious to have, as soon as the glad spring should come; and he wisely determined to take to himself a wife. I dare say he quite agreed with the present fashion of early marriages.

If we may credit Master Redbreast's own account of himself, he was exceedingly particular, and difficult to please; he prided himself on being descended from a long line of warriors; certainly, at times he was very quarrelsome and pugnacious, and would have found fault with a straw, if that straw chanced to lay in his way. Perhaps the fact of his feeling so much alone made him testy and cross; and so he seriously decided on looking about among all the neighbouring Redbreast gentry, who had unmarried daughters, for a helpmeet, and to settle down quiet and orderly, as the head of a family ought to settle down.

One day our hero had been flying a long way over gardens, and fields, and barren moors, till at last he arrived at a tall dark wood, and perched down to rest his weary wing on a hawthorn bough, beneath which a little stream went trickling by, and where, to Master Redbreast's great delight, he could drink, and dress his soft brown feathers, after his fatiguing, dusty journey.

This little stream, which proved such a source of satisfaction to the tired bird, wandered playfully through beds of reeds and rushes; while, here and there, rugged stones, and blocks of trees, upon which grew the feathery grass, the tall fern, the slender maiden-hair, and the delicately-tinted lichen, stood in its way, and caused the pure waters to crest and foam, as if they were angry at being resisted.

On one side, a clump of stately ferns rose up to the river; and in the background a giant oak mingled its dark and varied hues, as the soft breezes of spring gently waved their young and tender branches, or now and then wafted a withered leaf into the pretty rivulet at its feet.

A few steps to the right, and a few yards down the stream, crossed by a bridge, there stood a small thatched cottage, its walls ready to tumble down with age and neglect. A few broken stones, which once served as steps, were still before the door; but they only spoke of danger and risk to any one venturesome enough to " set foot" on them.

Notwithstanding the desolate aspect of the place, the soft coo, coo, of the pretty wood pigeon, as she sat on a tough bough of the old oak tree, enjoying the sweet perfume of the wild thyme, which was just peeping above the ground, fell on the air.

> Oh! this world is full of beauty,
> As the starry one above;
> And if we but did our duty,
> It would be a world of love!

In the midst of all this varied scenery, our friend, Master Redbreast, very unromantically went to sleep! I don't know if he snored or not, but if he did, he would never " own to it."

How long his slumbers lasted, or what kind of dreams he had, I do not know; but all at once he was roused by a pretty chirp and twitter close to his ear; and opening his bright eye, he saw a sweet little Lady Redbreast, drinking from the clear stream I have just mentioned. He watched her for some time; and the longer he looked, the more he admired her graceful shape and sparkling eye.

As he gazed, he perceived that the little lady suddenly looked frightened, and uttered a sharp chirp, as a carter's boy came on, smacking his great whip, and whistling loudly, as he led his horses to water; upon which she flew, affrighted, to the refuge of the hawthorn bough, and seemed ready to drop. In all probability she would have done so, had not Master Redbreast gallantly flown to her, and perched himself by her side, as much as to say, " Don't be terrified, dear little lady, I will protect you ;" whereupon she chirped a little note of thanks.

When the horses had splashed about in the water to their hearts' content, they plodded home, and all was quiet once more. A few steady-going cows were coming slowly towards the rivulet; the long branches of the oak drooped almost to the ground.

The gorgeous streaks of the setting sun were reflected on the still bosom of the stream, and all the symptoms of coming night warned little Lady Redbreast that she must betake herself to the thatch of the tumble-down cottage for shelter and repose; she therefore chirped three soft tender chirps, as if to say, " Good-night, my kind protector," and flew towards the thatch.

The next day our friend found no grubs so fine, no waters so refreshing, no flowers so sweet as those of the little running stream; and he lingered, and lingered about the place, while, strange to say, the little lady bird did the same; though she never chirped even one small chirp of encouragement when he looked towards her; she was a modest, retiring little Miss, and I like her for that.

On the second day, just as the bright sun began to kiss the dew drops off the wild thyme and the daisies, Master Redbreast summoned up all his courage, and asked the little lady to be his wife.

She was singing, at that moment, a small plaintive song, at the extreme twig of the hawthorn bough: he told her he was quite sure he could keep her in comfort; he was active and industrious,—in short, one of those early birds who catch the worm. He was a *water-drinker too,* and so should not waste his time, and his health, and his energies, but live comfortably at home with his wife and his children.

I don't think it would be quite fair to listen to all that passed; for most likely Master Redbreast felt somewhat awkward and bashful. Not **that** I ever heard of a bashful Redbreast—they are generally bold and brave enough; but it seems natural he should be a little put out on this novel occasion.

Then a debate apparently took place, and I suppose there will be no harm if I just fancy what passed between them! "And where shall we make our nest, sweet **love**?" gently asks the bridegroom elect; and as his little bride, that was to be, did not reply, he continued, in a hurried manner, "not by the stream, for *there* the rude carter-boy frightened you—and not in the old barn yonder, for I saw a large white cat stand looking up at you last evening—and not too near the road, or cruel heartless boys——"

Just at this point of his discourse, Master Redbreast was very unceremoniously interrupted by the notes of silvery bells, which pealed from the tower of a beautiful old church, not far from where they were perched.

Very pleasant and merrily sounded those notes in the distance. I shouldn't wonder if Redbreast thought something about wedding bells! By and bye, a group of children, with books in their hands, and others with bags slung over their shoulders, went running joyously past them.

They were nice-looking, clean, fair-haired youngsters; and two of them, who were lagging a short distance behind the rest, caught sight of our dear little Redbreasts. "Oh, look! oh look at those pretty robins, Jane!" "I wish they would go with us," exclaimed little Annie Johnston. "Come on, and get your ticket like a good girl," replied careful Jane. Annie looked wistfully at the robins, and called out, "Bobby! Bobby! pretty Bobby!" whereupon "Bobby" chirped, and Annie chirped too, in imitation of "Bobby."

Then "Bobby" looked kindly at his little wife, and she seemed to understand his looks; for they both immediately flew a few steps in advance, which so delighted Annie, that she trotted on by her sister's side, until, coming to the village, the pretty Bobbies both flew away, and alighted on the bough of the old yew-tree, which grew among the joints of the stone-work of the church tower in a very remarkable manner.

It was, and always had been, a source of great "wonderment" among the good people of the village how this yew tree ever came into such an exalted position. Most probably some little bird, long, long ago, dropped a seed from his mouth, as he flew over the place, and so it took root, and sprang up.

For my own part, I never could look at the famous old tree, but it reminded me of the "seed" of God's blessed Word, which the loving Saviour spoke about so often.

Can any of my little readers get the Bible, and find out the passage? It will well repay them for the time they spare.

Well! only fancy, the bough I have been telling you about is growing out of the dear old church tower at this very day, and is a fine sheltered refuge for the little feathered tribes in the summer from the heat, and in winter from the cold; and, behold! on one of the prettiest sprays, close together are perched Mr. and Mrs. Redbreast, the newly-married pair. They were

Mrs. Redbreast, the newly married pair, they are looking down at the village children as they passed merrily on, singing and laughing in the innocent gaiety of their sorrowless hearts.

The day after is the quiet Sabbath; and our little friends watch the congregation, as, one after another, they arrive. They recognise, too, many of the merry children they saw the day before at their games; but now they are very steady and subdued.

By and by, the strains of the old church organ pealed solemnly over the bright air, and then young voices helped to swell the song of praise ascending to the gracious and merciful God, who clothes the earth in its beauty and fertility, and who cares alike for all.

After the people were gone out of church, our dear robins flew to an adjoining garden. How peaceful and quiet it all was! The shrubs so green! The ivy so fresh! Opposite to where they perched, there was a window filled with dear prattling children, who were amusing themselves by pointing to the brilliant and many-coloured flowers which grew in abundance before them.

C

By and bye, their quick, bright eyes lighted on **Mr.**
and Mrs. Robin, and immediately they began to call
"Bobby! Bobby!" while one darling child ran into
the kitchen, and brought back a quantity of crumbs,
evidently "saved up" for feeding birds, and scattered
them coaxingly towards our hero and heroine. I
scarcely need tell you that they required no second
invitation; down they flew, confiding in the gentle
children perched close to the window, and made a
most substantial and delicious repast.

After they had dined, they hopped about, and sang
some soft little notes, just as if to say, "Thank you!
thank you! sweet little ones, for taking thought of us!
Thank you! thank you! gentle children; much we love
you all."

As the shades of evening began to cast the old
church tower into a solemn gloom, the loving pair
crept into some thick, dark ivy, which grew round the
nursery window at the rectory, and there they slept
snugly and safely.

On the following morning, seeing the church doors
open, they flew inside. All was hushed and still.
First, they perched on the curious old stone font; then

they flew a little further up the aisle, and lighted on an old lady's large brass-clasped prayer-book; and finally, they both hopped into the reading desk, and there nestled close together in the scarlet cloth that covered it. Long time they remained in this spot, laying their little heads together, and twittering, just as if they were holding a conversation on some very important subject.

A celebrated French philosopher once gave his opinion, that birds really had a language of their own; and I don't see any reason why this may not be the case; at any rate, there is no harm in my just fancying the discourse that took place between them on the present occasion.

Nestling close to her dear husband, little Mrs. Redbreast thus exclaims, " Oh, my own dear Robin, what a quiet, lovely spot this is! I seem to have no fear of anything here. I should like to live in this fine large house with you for ever; I should never care to go anywhere else."

"It is a beautiful house indeed, my darling; and where could we find a spot more safe to build our nest, and rear our little ones?" replied Robin; and he looked proudly and fondly at his own dear *wee* wife.

"And we are close to the house where those tender-hearted children live," continued Mrs. Robin; "and they will never be cruel to us, and steal our eggs, or rob us of our young ones;" and here she gave a shudder, as if she had seen unfeeling, hard-hearted, monster boys torture the little half-fledged chirping nestlings for their amusement, as I have often seen them.

Robin pressed his wing close to her side, as he replied, "I am sure *those* children will never frighten you! **Did** you see their bright eyes dance and glisten, as they threw us out those delicious crumbs? And what curly heads two of them have! I quite love them already, and hope we shall often see them **in** this beautiful house. Suppose we hop all about everywhere, and see if we can find a spot for our nest," continued Robin, after a pause.

To this very wise suggestion the *wee* wife consented; and away they flew to the organ loft. Neither of them fancied this exalted position, so they flew and perched **on** an old hatchment, which had been hanging in the church for many long years. **This** spot did not seem to suit, and they flew down on the floor, and hopped **about** for nearly **an hour,** as if looking for what they could not find.

At length they alighted on the communion table, and here they remained for a considerable time; but Mrs. Robin could not help casting sundry longing glances back to the reading desk, which Robin perceiving, he proposed that they should return thither; to which she joyfully assented, and back they flew, both agreeing that "no spot on earth could be better for their nest."

On the desk there lay the large well-worn **Bible,** out of whose sacred pages many a word of hope, and peace, and comfort had fallen on world-weary hearts. Its polished massive clasps were lightly closed, and **a** space left between its leaves and the side of the desk.

Into this cunning little nook they stole, and there **they** built their **nest!** Oh! how busily they set **to** work. First a bit of matting from the churchwarden's pew; **then** a fragment of wool which they picked off the end **of** an ancient piece of carpet in old Dame Glaze's "seat;" then a thread off the hassock in the **desk** itself!

All at once they flew out of a window which was left
open, and came to an old moat close by. Here they
picked up a number of soft brown leaves to line their
nest, and make it comfortable for their precious nestlings.

While they were "stopping to rest," after having
flown, laden with leaves, several times back **to their**
nest, they were attracted by a great many guinea fowls,
and other poultry, that had wandered away from the
old manor house, and were enjoying their feathering
on the banks of the somewhat muddy moat.

Oh! what treasures, and treasures they found!
Hair of all lengths and colour, which fell from the
sleek black cow and her companions, Cherry, Daisy,
Buttercup, and Strawberry, as they cooled themselves
beside the moat, with the old cart horses, Smiler,
Boxer, Dobbin, and Leader; and how they collected
and carried them home to their nest!

Thus cleverly, and delightfully, the happy birds set
to work, and who so proud as they?

By and **bye**, the dinner bell at the rectory began to
ring, and Robin remarked to his wife, "I think that

bell seems to say, ' Come, Robins, come !' " whereupon his wife quite agreed with him, as all good wives should, when their husbands make sensible remarks; so away they flew down the gravel walk of the old churchyard, over the green shrubs, and at once perched boldly, as only redbreasts can, on the sill of the nursery window.

Here a hearty welcome awaited them. The moment the dear little rectory children had finished their dinners, they scattered all along the sill quantities of cake crumbs, from which Bobbies made a most refreshing meal, and again flew back to their work. As nothing occurred to disturb their proceedings, their nest was soon completed.

On the following Sabbath, when the good rector went into the church, as was his custom, some time before the hour at which divine service commenced, he entered the desk, and having reverently placed his hand on the Bible, what was his amazement to find, close to his fingers, a beautiful nest, and a dear little robin peeping at him with her bright, sparkling bead-like eyes!

Only fancy, my dear young readers, the surprise of the good clergyman! Nor was his surprise at all lessened by the fact that the bird sat quietly on her nest, never attempting to fly away, just as much as to say, "Ah! my good friend, I am not afraid of *you*. I can see something **in** your kind face that reminds me of those darling little curly-headed children at the rectory, and what have I to fear?"

The rector had scarcely recovered from his first amazement, when a few notes, very sweet and very soft, caught his ear; and looking up in the direction from whence they came, he saw Master Robin perched on one of the gilt pipes of the organ, chanting, as it seemed to him, a morning hymn of praise.

Deeply touched, not only by the song of the little warbler, but by the quiet watching of his little wife, the beautiful verse from the eighty-fourth Psalm came involuntarily into the rector's thoughts, "*Yea, the sparrow hath found an house, and the swallow a nest for herself, where she may lay her young, even thine altar, O Lord of hosts, my King and my God!*"

He walked softly out of the desk, and remarked to

the aged man, the parish clerk, who came up at that moment, "George, you must not on any account go into the reading desk this morning to find out the lessons;" and he then told him about the little **nest,** and his own earnest wish that it should not be discovered, or the bird molested.

Always after this, the clergyman brought his own Bible, and read the lessons from it, so that she should not **be** disturbed, and he also took a white silk handkerchief, and threw it over the end of the large book, **thus** protecting his little favourite during the time of divine service; and truly she seemed as if nothing earthly could scare or frighten her: she felt she was under the eye of a friend.

Time passed on. One little speckled egg appeared, then another, and another, until four *wee* beauties were **laid** in the nest. And was not Mr. Robin a proud **bird** now, and was not Mrs. Robin as happy as the days were long, while they gazed tenderly on their treasures, and thought on the time when, from these speckled **dots,** would come forth their longed-for little ones.

Day by day, all the wants of the parent birds were carefully supplied by their kind friends ; the faithful wife seldom leaving her eggs, lest they should become cold, and her young ones die in their shells.

Robin was equally anxious about them, and for the health of his wife. He was most attentive in waiting upon her, constantly bringing her tit-bits from the rectory, and all the greenest grass he could pick up ; and when she was thirsty he would take her place, and keep the eggs warm, while she went out to the edge of the moat, and drank to quench her thirst.

Then he would enliven her with many a merry ditty and lively song, and while away the long hours by planning their future life, what they would do, and where they would go ; how they would bring up their children, and try to make them good, obedient, gentle, loving. Evidently Robin thought it much better to be useful, in however humble a way, than living in idleness and luxury.

The peacock is a handsome bird enough, but I really think the little robin redbreast is a greater favourite. I remember, when a child, learning some verses, commencing

Little bird, with bosom red,
Welcome to our humble shed;
Daily round my table steal,
While I eat my scanty meal;
Doubt not, little though there be,
But I'll find a crumb for thee.

I recollect too, a lady telling me a very interesting little incident, which occurred in her own house, showing the love and wondrous sagacity of these dear birds. Returning from a walk one morning, my friend found a poor little nestling redbreast, which had either been ducked in the water by cruel boys, or had fallen into a pool, for it was wet and miserable. So she took it tenderly up in her warm hand, carried it home, put it into a small basket, and laid it down in the sunshine, which shone brightly on the carpet.

In a few moments, two redbreasts flew into the room and perched on the rim of the basket; after watching a short time, they flew out of the room and returned again, each bearing in its mouth food for the little sufferer; they stayed some time looking down upon it, and then flew away again.

The next morning they came again, each carrying a worm, which they dropped into the basket, and re-mained a longer time. When they returned in the evening **their** nestling **was dead**; and they **flew away** instantly, and never returned again. Evidently **they** knew it was *dead*. *How?*

But, dear **me**! dear me! I have wandered away from Mr. and Mrs. Robin! Pray forgive me, dear child, and I'll try not to offend in the same way again.

CHAPTER III.

"He prayeth best, who loveth best
Both man, and bird, and beast;
For the dear God, who loveth us,
He made and loveth all."

I MUST now return for a moment to the old church, shaded with its dark yew tree, looking so solemn and picturesque; the hedges round about are cut in the old-fashioned style—very stiff and stupid I think— shaped into such curious devices. In the said dear old church there sat Mrs. Robin on her throne, from whence she could see the little pathway through the churchyard. And that was, indeed, a sight to make one pause and *think*.

Oh! how many graves were scattered around,—tiny, very tiny ones,—with their "daisy quilt;" the gentle flower reminding the beholder that the tender babe had left the cold world to bloom in everlasting sunshine. There was **one** spot that **I** always lingered near. It seemed to **speak to** me—

> " It died! for Adam sinned ;
> It lives, **for** Jesus died!"

I would always fancy the darling babe safely nestled **in the** bosom of the **Good** Shepherd, "*who laid down his life for his sheep.*"

There were other graves, but **I** must not stay longer **to** tell of them, but just remark, that as our friend **Mrs.** Robin **sat** in the desk, she **could** see numbers of **the villagers** pass and re-pass; **and** now and then she could **catch** a few words of their conversation.

Some would be talking **of** the weather and the crops ; **others,** about the last " news " in the village ; **and** a few would speak **of** the goodness **of** God, in clothing the earth with **so** much beauty **and** richness. Pity this subject **is not more** the theme **of** discourse !

As **I** was saying, **there** sat faithful, patient little Mrs. **Robin** ; and at **length** all her watchful care was rewarded ; **all** her anxieties were **at** an end. First **one,** then another, and then a third, and a fourth little

bird cracks its shell, **and** out pops its naked *wee* head ;
and they were soon, one after another, sheltered under
her warm wing, and with a low **sleepy chirp, which
filled** her heart with joy and gladness, they soon closed
their tender eyes, and went off into a sweet slumber ;
while Mr. Robin, perched on the pulpit above their
heads, sings his grandest song in honour of the auspi-
cious event.

Soon came the important question, " What are their
names to be ?" The eldest was called " Bobby," being
an old family name ; the second " Whistle," because,
like many other fond mothers, Mrs. Robin thought her
son had a very superior voice ; then the oldest daughter was called " Miss Chirp," and the youngest, **being**
somewhat delicate, " Weeney."

A busy time now began for the youthful father and
mother. Their young ones were hungry little birds,
who never seemed satisfied. Their yellow beaks were
always wide open, except when they were asleep ; and
there was a great demand for spiders **and** flies, on the
part of Mr. Robin.

High living, and no exercise **or care, soon** made

them grow strong and hearty. Master Bobby was the flower of the flock, as regards his personal appearance, but he was by no means the best behaved. He was proud of being the eldest, and soon began to show unamiable, quarrelsome propensities, which gave his parents great uneasiness.

While his mother was at home, he was obliged to content himself with only a sly push, or a secret peck at poor little Weeney, of whom he was jealous, because, being delicate, she sometimes got an extra grub, or a few more crumbs; but as soon as his mother's back was turned, and she accompanied their father in search of food,—which search was falling too heavily on him—goodness! what a dust Master Bobby would kick up!

The nest seemed too small for his grandeur, and he would push, and push, and push, till he had pushed the others to the edge of the nest; and then he would peck to the right and left like a feathered Nero. A pity he never learnt that nice little verse of good Dr. Watts, commencing—

"Birds in their little nests agree—"

I dare say you know the hymn, my dear young reader.
It is generally among the first pieces children learn,
and there are few prettier or wiser.

One day Robin came home very tired indeed. There
had been a scarcity of flies and other dainties, on account of a long drought; and the next morning, like a
dutiful, affectionate wife, Mrs. Robin determined **to**
leave him at home **to take care of** the young ones,
while she went in search of supplies.

Robin very reluctantly consented to this, but, over-
persuaded by her he loved so well, he yielded the point,
and **allowed** her to go.

Before **she** left the nest, however, she **gave** all her
children **a** kind motherly word of admonition. **I can**
fancy I hear her saying, **" Bobby, you are the** eldest,
and should be kind and good-natured to your young
brothers and sisters, who naturally look up to you for
an example. Never be selfish, wanting the softest
place **in the** nest, and the nicest piece to eat, which of
course **leads** to wrangling and quarrelling. Above all,
my dear **boy**, Bobby, always be kind to poor sister

D

Weeney; she's not strong, and I am afraid I shall have trouble in bringing her up."

While she is making these kind remarks, her young ones are touched, and promise to attend to everything she wishes; they think her the best of mothers, and when she left them, and flew away out of sight, they nestled close together, and seemed very happy and peaceably inclined.

This state of things lasted only a short time. Master Bobby got tired of being good. He said he was hungry and chilly, so he began flapping his downy wings, as if *that* would be of any use! Then he opened his beak very wide, and stretched his legs so rudely, that they almost pushed Weeney out of the nest.

Chirp had been quietly reposing, but the plaintive voice of her poor little sister roused her, and she opened her eyes and looked very frightened. Just then, another and harder kick threw her on the extreme edge of the nest; and had not Whistle pushed her back with his wing, she would have fallen on the cold stones of the floor, and most likely broken one of her limbs, if it had not killed her outright. Now began **a** terrible uproar.

I ought to have remarked, in **order** to explain their being left alone, that when Mrs. Robin got out into the lovely air, **she** flew away further than she intended; thinking, kind creature that she was, "what a nice **rest** Robin would have."

As, therefore, **she did not** return at the very moment he expected her, he **began to get** fidgetty and uneasy; while sundry remembrances of carters' horses, cruel cats, and still crueller boys, came thronging upon him; so away he flew **in** search of his darling wife; which explains the children being left alone, as I before remarked.

Now, I repeat, began **a** sad uproar. Whistle gave an angry peck at Bobby for his unkindness to Weeney —**and** Bobby being much the stronger of the two, pecked him in return, till he cried out. Chirp set up a **loud** call for her mother, and poor Weeney sobbed piteously, **as** the fighting and noise went on.

To such **a** pitch had this uproar proceeded, that they neither of them heard the approach of their father;

and you may well fancy, my dear little readers, how grieved and surprised he was; so much so, indeed, that he let fall a most dainty mouthful he had brought to divide among them, hopped hastily into the nest, and demanded the cause of such a riot.

With ruffled feathers and angry eye, Master Bobby attempted to make his "own story good;" but he faltered and stammered so much, that his father easily saw that he was at his old work again, and severely reprimanded him for his conduct.

"Oh, Bobby," I can fancy I hear him say, "Oh, Bobby! how can you be so unkind to your little brother and sisters, who love you, and never would say a word to you, if you did not begin at them? And how came you to be so ungrateful to your dear mother, who watched over you with such care and tenderness? Your behaviour will break her heart, as it almost does mine;" and here the distressed father sighed, and a tear stood in his bright eye.

The conduct of this refractory bird should be a warning to my little readers, if they ever indulge in selfishness towards their brothers and sisters, or disobey, and thus vex and grieve their dear parents.

Ask yourself, now, dear child, "Have I not often given way to angry words and feelings? Have I not often coveted either my schoolfellows' place, or something they had which I had not, and given cross, envious looks? Have I not sometimes been tempted to tell a falsehood—forgetting that the eye of the Great God was upon me, and His ear open to all I say?" Then, too, have I not forgotten the words of the loving Saviour, who says to little children, as well as to grown-up people, "*Learn of me, for I am meek and lowly in heart.*"

Oh! my child, never give way to angry words, and evil tempers; for when you do, you grieve this kind and loving Saviour, who cares for you, and gave His precious life to save you from "going down to the pit."

In returning to our friends, the robins, I would observe, that you may be sure when their mother came home, she, too, was greatly pained; and to punish Bobby for his bad conduct, she put him as far as she possibly could from her, and kept him without his supper; so he was obliged to lie hungry and cold all the night.

This wholesome reproof did him good for a day or two ; he did not very well like being kept without food, and put out at the edge of the nest all night; but alas! he was such a naughty **bird** in his heart, that he secretly determined, as soon as he was old enough, to run away from the nest, and **go** where he liked, and do just as he pleased.   We shall see the result of **this** self-will and disobedience.

One morning, about ten days after the quarrel just recorded—and a lovely morning it was—the sun, glittered **on the** old church **clock, shed its** bright beams through the chancel window, and little threads of light sparkled through the great key-holes of the knotted doors like diamonds.

All looked **so** bright, so warm, that Mr. Robin proposed to indulge the children by taking them a hop round the church.   To this Mrs. Robin readily consented, and in a few moments out bustled Bobby, glad to escape from the nest.

Out stepped Whistle, cheerful as a cricket, and Chirp had just got on the edge of the nest, when she saw that her little sister, Weeney, was not strong enough to accompany her; so she called to her mother, and asked if she might "stay with poor dear sister Weeney, as she would be so very dull at home alone."

Very glad indeed was little Weeney to hear this request. How dearly she loved her kind, unselfish sister! How closely she nestled up to her, and put her little beak up to be kissed!

The day certainly **did** seem long, and sometimes kind Chirp could not help thinking of the pleasure her brothers were having; but she would not allow these thoughts to get the better of her; she checked them at once.

On Mrs. Robin's return, she brought them one of the nicest dinners ever little birds could have had; and they both enjoyed it amazingly, especially Chirp, who had the approval of her own conscience; and this heightens *all* pleasures, or, rather, there can be no *real* pleasure without it.

She felt she had done right, and when she put her head under her wing, and went to sleep that night, a happy bird was she, and pleasant were her dreams about Weeney, whom she fancied strong and well, hopping by her side, and singing as loud and cheerful as the best of them. Kind, dear Chirp !

My little reader, is this your constant practice ? Are you willing to give up your own wishes, to please a sick sister, or a delicate brother ? Never forget, that in doing good to others, you insure happiness on yourself. Not that you should do good for the sake of this, but it is the natural result.

Nothing remarkable occurred to Bobby, or Whistle on the first day of their leaving their nest. The presence of their father acted as a check on the former, and he dared not show off his quarrelsome propensities ; so he contented himself with devouring every fly and moth within his reach ; while his brother kindly put several dainty tit-bits aside, intending to carry them home to his sisters ; but greedy Bobby soon caught sight of them, and gobbled them up in no time. This greediness so displeased his father, that he would not give him any instruction in the art of carrying grubs or flies in his beak to a distance ; while he gratified Whistle, by not only showing him how to do so, but also let him take one home to Weeney, which highly delighted his generous nature. There was not a trace of greediness in *his* character. Can you say the same, dear little reader?

Time passed away, and the young family of **the** Robins were getting quite strong; they could hop almost "like papa." It was Whistle's great ambition to resemble his kind, good father. They could also use their wings fearlessly, and their tail feathers were growing famously. These circumstances, added to the fact of their finding the nest too small, now their young ones were rapidly growing bigger, induced Mr. **and** Mrs. Robin to decide on removing to more extensive quarters.

They were all delighted with a prospect of change: Bobby, because he would be more at liberty to do as he pleased, and Whistle, because he began to grow very proud of his voice; while the Misses Chirp and Weeney, had a little lingering to see the world, of which they had **got** some idea, **from** hearing their brothers talking over what they had seen.

One evening Mrs. Robin was a great deal behind her usual time of returning; and naturally they all began to get very uneasy, especially Robin himself, whose affection for his wife seemed to "grow with his growth;" **and** he was just **on** the point of flying off to seek for her, when in she flew very fast, and apparently agitated. After pausing to take breath, she informed them that she had been detained at the rectory by the only enemy she had there, in the shape of the children's pet cat!

Begging Mrs. Robin's pardon for interrupting her, I must first say a word or two about this said cat; for *she* seems **to** understand all about her; my little readers do *not.* So I will just say that "Dora" was a general favourite all over the house, not only for her fine sleek tortoise-shell coat, and magnificent tail, but because she was known as a well behaved cat, with the exception of her being over fond of poor little sparrows and robins. Very tame and affectionate too was this Dora; she followed the family about like a little dog, **and** would sit on her kind master's shoulder, while **he** read the newspaper after breakfast; and sometimes **if** he read longer than usual, in order to attract his attention, she would give him sundry little pats, and place her paw on the paper, as much as to say, " Please leave off reading, dear master, and let me have a walk in the garden. "

I am afraid—to speak the truth—that Dora was **a** spoilt, indulged **cat;** and like most spoilt creatures, children and all, she was apt to be a wee bit disagreeable ; not that she herself was aware of it, and I verily believe that the dear **Robins** need not have been at all frightened about **her.** **She** was too happy, too well cared **for** to mind them just then, not having kittens to give the young ones to, to amuse them.

With all Dora's agreeable ways (and the darling rectory **children** thought there never was such a cat **as** theirs) she had one trick, which had grown into an incorrigible habit from indulgence. She could never pass the dairy door without looking in ; and frequently she did *more* than look in, if the state of her whiskers, and the wiping of her lips with her paws might be taken **as** an evidence against her.

But **I** have wandered unpardonably away from dear Mrs. Robin. By way of rewarding **her,** I will let her tell her own story :—" Well, my dears," she continued,

" I thought that when I was out, I might just as well
pay a little visit to the cook at the rectory, who was
always so good-natured, **and** not cross, as cooks generally are.   You recollect, Robin, dear, how handsomely
she used to treat us ?   Well, as I was saying, I just
hopped upon, and sat **on** the scullery window ; when,
all of a sudden, I heard such a splashing, **and** mewing !
it made me shake and tremble all over **like an** aspen
leaf ; for I expected every moment to be eaten up alive.
Good-natured cook ran as fast as she could towards
the dairy ; no doubt she was accustomed to such
sounds ; **and at** that very moment **her** mistress happened to be passing, and she **ran in too.**   Then I took
courage and flew down to see what was the **matter.**
Oh ! what a sight met my eye !   There, in the large
round cream pan, nearly full of thick rich cream—for
it was churning day—there, kicking, and struggling,
and mewing—there, quite a pitiable spectacle to behold—lay our only rectory enemy, Madam Dora !

With difficulty the selfish creature **was** lifted out ; her
fine fur coat, which she is so proud **of,** sticking closely
to her skin ; her grand tail all heavy with the cream ;

her eyes shut, and her whole figure looking as miserable and ridiculous as you can imagine. Notwithstanding her bad behaviour, I saw her kind mistress wipe
off the cream from her coat, wrap her up in a warm
shawl, until she could obtain some hot water; and then
she washed her carefully, and laid her in a warm box,
and told her to "go to sleep like a good cat." But
depend upon it, my dear Robin," she continued,
turning to her husband, "the greedy creature has
taken a violent cold, and wont be out again for one
while; so we will avail ourselves of her absence, and
take out our children to-morrow."

After a remark or two from Mr. Robin, expressive
of his admiration at the discernment and good sense of
his little wife, Mrs. Robin turned to Bobby, and in a
gentle, affectionate tone, thus addressed him: "Ah,
my dear boy, let the misfortune that has thus fallen on
this greedy Dora be a warning to you. Self-will, and
disobedience always bring disgrace of some kind.
Now, for a long time, the cat's fur will smell very
badly from the cream; and she will be shut out of her
nice snug quarters on the drawing-room rug. As to

the nursery, I am pretty sure that Mrs. Nurse wont allow those **dear**, clean little children **to** have anything **to do** with her, the nasty creamy thing! Had she been contented **with** her usual good fare, this sad misfortune would never have happened to her. Therefore remember, **my** dear children, **that** moderation **has** its own reward, and that intemperance ever **brings its own** punishment."

Scarcely had Mrs. Robin finished her excellent advice, **and her** young ones were busy in talking over **what** she **had** said, when **a** tremendous noise was heard—sh**uffling** and scuffling **of** feet—and then such a loud **blow! they** thought **surely the** windows were coming in; **but** nothing **of the kind.** It was only Dick Wilful and Harry Mischief going home **from** school, quarrelling and throwing stones, as they **usually** did, **when** one unlucky stone **went** the wrong **way,** and shot through a window of **the church,** close **by** poor Robin's nest. **Then** the mischievous young monkeys, on seeing the damage they **had** done, took to their heels, and ran towards home as fast **as** they could, hoping and believing that no one had seen them. They then became good friends, and resolved to say nothing about the broken window.

When these bad boys laid down their heads to sleep that night, they neither of them thought or cared anything about having disobeyed their schoolmaster's commands, "never to play in the churchyard, nor to throw stones at all." They did not imagine that any **one saw** them. To escape punishment was the **only** thing they cared for. "Ah!" thought they, "we shall not be found out; nobody saw us throw the stones, and what do **we care** if they did?" Wicked boys! they had **often been** taught at the Sunday School, that they could never, *never* escape the **eye** of God; that His Almighty eye

> "Strikes through the shades of night;
> And **our most** secret actions lie
> All open **to** His sight."

But **they** were seen **of *man*** also, though they little thought **so**. The schoolmaster was walking in a neighbour's garden close by, and saw them throw, and heard the crash of the breaking window.

The next morning they marched boldly into the school-room, and began to prepare their books. All seemed to be going on well for a time. By and bye, the boys were about to be dismissed, when Dick whispered to Harry, "We're safe enough now, Harry!" But—not so fast. Wait a moment, and you will see. Hark! The master shouts out in a loud voice, "Every boy remain in his place!" Dick turned pale, and looked at Harry, who was frightened enough. Their consciences told them something was coming. A painful silence ensued; then the master exclaimed, "Dick Wilful and Harry Mischief, come forward!"

The two culprits, thus addressed, were ready to sink into their very shoes with fear. Slowly and sullenly they moved on, for they dared not disobey; and they could not run away now. With a firm grasp on each boy's shoulder, the master then relates, in the presence of the whole school, what these idle boys had done— how they had disobeyed his strict commands, alike heedless of his displeasure, or the consequences of their wickedness. He then gave them a severe caning, which they richly deserved; and no one pitied them.

They were known in the school as a pair of idle, hardened boys, who led away the younger ones into mischief. So none of their schoolmates felt for them when they cried out, and made a great uproar, each time the cane fell over their shoulders and sides. I should think the pain they suffered taught them a lesson, and brought to their memories the agonies they had often inflicted on poor dumb animals and insects.

There was scarcely a dog **or** cat in the village that did **not** know them, and shrink away affrighted from them. On one occasion, they tied an old tin saucepan to a **string**, and fastened it to a dog's tail, and drove him, yelling and bleeding, **all over** the place, till **the** poor beast nearly went mad. At another time **they** caught a little kitten, just come outside a cottage door to sun itself, and after holding it under water, in a neighbouring pond, **till** it was half dead, they piled up a heap of dirt, and put it on the top of the pile, and **threw** stones at it till they hit its brains out, and it died in **great** torture.

But especially did these miserable boys delight in bird-nesting, and wringing the necks of the little ten-

E

der nestlings; and in tormenting those helpless insects,
known as cockchaffers.   They would even appoint **to**
meet one another, and try and bring some more boys,
as cruel as themselves, **to** "enjoy the fun" of seeing the
agony of the poor insect, as it spun round and round,
with a pin run through **its** little quivering body!

Remonstrating one day with these young monsters,
and telling them that God would assuredly punish
their sinful practices, one of them told me "cockchaffers didn't feel!" and asked me how I knew they
suffered pain?   I replied by taking a long pin from
my shawl, and requesting **the boy** to allow me **to**
pierce **it** through one of his fingers.   From this trial
of course **he** shrank; for **you** know, dear reader, the
cruel boy is *ever* a coward.

I then proposed to tell one of our **men**, who was
turning over hay in a field close by, to bring his bright
fork, and run it through the boy's body ; but at this he
turned pale, and fancying perhaps that I was about to
carry **my** lesson into practice, he took to his heels, and
ran bellowing home, as fast as he could !

I do think, that cruel and unfeeling as many boys

are, if they only knew but a little, a *very* little, of the torture they inflict, they would shrink from inflicting it on any of these poor harmless creatures, who are unable to speak a word, and to cry out for mercy. Their helplessness, of itself, ought to appeal to the heart of every boy who has one spark of kindness in his nature.

I knew a dear boy, who, whenever he saw a creature, formed by the hand of his heavenly Father, ill-used, would rush to the rescue, and plead, even with tears, for its release. Now, think you this lad, and a little lad he was too, was "chicken-hearted," and a "blubber head?" No! no!

Out upon the great world of waters, there rode a stately ship; every sail was unfurled to catch the breeze; every heart bounded cheerfully as she cut her way, as a bird cleaves the air with her snowy wing, through the crested waves, each bound bringing her nearer the wished-for "land." Anon, the scene changed! Suddenly, almost as a flash of lightning, the wind flew round; clouds covered the sky.

In less time than it takes me to tell you, dear children, every man was at his post, every sail was furled,

and they waited the rush of the squall.   Onward it
came, sweeping, sweeping with a death howl. Suddenly there was a quick movement to one side of the
gallant ship ; then yelled that terrible shout, that God
grant none of you may ever hear!—" Man overboard !"
To launch the friendly life boat, to leap into her with a
speed and energy, as if they were going to some glory
awaiting them, was but the work of an instant ; twelve
gallant fellows, and one brave boy—the *first* who
bounded into the boat—bearded the angry billows, to
try and save their fellow-man.   Like a black speck,
now on the top of a crested wave, then hid from sight
by its furious lashing—did that poor fellow seem to
their straining eyes.

With every noble nerve strung to its master pitch,
onward they speed ; and oh! joy! joy! they rapidly
near the drowning sailor!   "Another pull my hearties,
and we shall have him," shouted a firm, but youthful
voice.   Another pull, and they are close upon victory !
With **the** speed of the young panther leaping to its
mother's breast, did the sailor boy—whose shout, " another pull,.my hearties," had cheered on the rowers—

spring over the boat side, and grasp the desperate swimmer.

A wild hurrah! rose from the boat; a dozen sturdy arms were stretched out to cradle the rescuer, and the rescued. Then a great billow struck the boat, and drove her furiously on one side, leaving many yards between them and her crew! Oh! it was **a** dreadful moment! but all was not **lost.**

"God help the brave lad!" reverently exclaimed an old white-haired man; and a deep hoarse "Amen" followed. **Once** more the crew approach the struggling pair, and it was plainly to be seen that the brave boy could not much longer keep **his** grasp of the failing man. "God bless the boy!" again broke from the old sailor, as he watched the fearful conflict against the proud waves. Another moment, and again they closed upon them! Another moment, **and** they are both enclosed in the sailor's friendly arms!

But alas! alas! as they were dragging them in, the fair temple of the brave young saviour of his shipmate came **in** contact with a piece of iron, and a deadly wound opened its red lips, and poured forth his warm life-blood; and ere they could row back to their ship, the pale face, and shortened breathing of their favourite, as he lay in the bottom of the boat, by the side of his exhausted mate, filled those rowers with terrible anxiety. "If they could but reach her!" Oh! how they pulled, till their nerves seemed cracking! At last they gain the friendly bark. Tenderly they lift out the youthful pair; but who can paint the grief that sat on each manly face, as the ship surgeon shook his head, while he leant over the white upturned face of the bleeding boy!

After tending the wound, and forcing him to swallow a cordial, he seemed to revive a little, and opened his dark blue eyes with a sweet smile. The old sailor brushed off the tears that rolled down his face with the cuff of his jacket—bent down to him, and whispered to him. Once more he opened his beautiful eyes, and there shone a glory in them like the light of heaven; and from his pale and parted lips, he just murmured a few words—none who heard them ever forgot—"Captain of my salvation!"—and then he went to sleep, without a sigh or struggle.

The old sailor came from the same village as the

glorious sailor boy, and told all the solemn tale. And, my dear young readers, you perhaps would like to know the name of this hero.` Perhaps you have already guessed? Yes, you are right. It was no other than he they ridiculed as "chicken-heart," and "blubber-head." These coarse torturers of insects and animals! Ah! I wish every village boy, and every town and country boy too, was such a "chicken-heart," and "blubber-head," as the boy hero!

I have not told you the secret of all his loveliness of character. It was this. He had a dear mother, who loved her Saviour; and when he was a little curly headed, bright-browed, tender-hearted child, she used to call him to her knee, and tell him the story of that Saviour's love, till he learnt to love Him too; and when he went to sea, as a midshipman in one of the Queen's grand ships, his mother whispered in his willing ear, "My son never forsake the Captain of your salvation." "Never, *never*, my own mother," he smiled, as his arms relaxed from her loving neck: and they parted—never to meet again, till she meets her sailor boy, wearing the crown of glory "that fadeth not away."

CHAPTER IV.

But dear me! dear me! how I have flown away from my darling robins! Let me see, where was I? O, I remember—where Dick Wilful, and Harry Mischief threw a large stone through one of the church windows, and got a "sound thrashing" for it too. Well, through this very hole our robins flew, the next morning, in search of a favourable spot, where they could make a fresh home for themselves and young family. To say the least, I believe they had a *little* hankering to see something more of the world than they had done since their marriage.

I suppose I need not repeat, that all the young ones, for reasons before stated, were anxious enough to change their quiet quarters. Very eagerly, therefore, did they look out on that bright summer morning, to see if "it was likely to keep fine;" and their anticipations were realized ; for a more lovely day never shone on the earth. Not a cloud dimmed the glad blue sky!

The cool green leaves whispered lovingly to each other. The **rivulet**, of which **I have spoken, went on** murmuring soft music. The very air seemed full of joy and praise, filled as it was with the perfume of flowers, and the songs of thousands of feathered musicians.

Our dear birdies, one and all, were nearly out of their wits with enjoyment. They hopped from bough to bough, chirping at the top of their voices from very happiness. I am sure that only the slender, dainty foot of a robin could have possibly rested on the delicate twigs they perched upon. Nothing *could* exceed their delight! Never had they seen anything so beautiful as the rectory garden! Never had they even dreamed of such fairy land, not they! And the butterflies! Oh, what butterflies! Their blue and gold wings, glittering in the sun's warm ray, almost blinded poor Weeney. The constant chorus from the other birds almost bewildered her. Even bold Bobby left off gormandizing some cake crumbs he fell in with, to look up, and admire all the beauties round about him; till at last, wearied with enjoyment, and lulled by **the** hum of thousands of " busy bees," they all four nestled together in the stump of an old tree, and went off fast asleep.

Seeing them so safely occupied, their good parents took the opportunity of making a friendly call on some very genteel robins, who had come to settle in an adjoining field, **and who long** wished to cultivate their friendship. After they had paid their visit, they flew to their old trysting place—the nursery window **at the** rectory—probably with some idea of learning the fate of cream-loving Dora, or of getting some "goodies" for their young ones from **the** dear curly-haired rectory children.

How **long** they remained away I cannot tell; for time passes very swiftly, especially in making "**morning calls**;" and how long their little ones slept **I am** equally ignorant; but, by and bye, Bobby opened first one eye, then the other, and looked all around. Then he called "Chirp! chirp!" meaning "Mother! mother!" and as no reply came, he laid down again and tried to get another "nap." As, however, he could not "forget himself" **in** that way, he speedily forgot himself in another way; so he gave his brother a pretty sharp

peck, for no reason in the world, but because he was
tired of being quiet and good. Whistle, however, being
too comfortable and sleepy to mind him, he shut up
his eyes, drooped his head on one side, and told him,
in a drowsy tone, to "be off, and mind his own busi-
ness."

It was pretty clear that Bobby caught an idea from
this rebuke of his brother; for he hopped about four
inches, intending to "be off." Then he hopped back
again, and gave poor slumbering Whistle another and
harder peck, and flew away "to mind his own busi-
ness," as he supposed, by making friends with the first
bird that came in his way.

Now I must just remark here, that this was one of
the warnings his wise mother had laid very strongly
on Bobby to observe, namely, to be very careful not to
make any street acquaintances. "Young birds," she
remarked, and I add, young people too, "are very fond
of believing they know a good deal better than their
parents in this respect." "O," say they, "I'm sure
there can't be any harm in this, or that; mother is so
particular, and nonsensical, just as if we didn't know

right from wrong,"—and so on. I dare say you will
think me very nonsensical too, when I say that is the
very point; you *don't* "know right from wrong." How
should you, young as you are?   You have no *experience* to guide you; and *wise* people are often deceived,
putting "sweet for bitter, **and** bitter for sweet." Therefore, ever remember the fifth commandment, to *honour*,
that is, *to obey your father and mother*. God never loves
a disobedient child; nay, more, God is angry with the
disobedient child every day.   Oh! how *dreadful* a
thing *that* is! And then, as to making acquaintances
in the streets, it never comes to any good; and so you
will see in the case of this self-willed, disobedient bird.

After, as I before said, giving his brother a sharp
peck, only to gratify his mischievous disposition, he
flew over a hedge, and lighted close to a young robin
who was looking for grubs in the field. In the boldest
manner Bobby thus began: "I say, old fellow, what
are you moping there all alone for?"

" And what were *you* moping for just now, 'long of
those young chirping things yonder?" retorted Master
Ruby, pertly.   Bobby was ashamed to say he had been

"napping;" he thought it would look so like a baby-bird; so he puffed himself out, and swelling with importance, like the ox in the fable, he replied, "I was entrusted by my father and mother, Mr. and Mrs. Robin, to take care of my young brother and sisters, while they went to dine with a family of distinction close by."

Ruby was a deep bird; he saw, at a glance, Bobby's weak points; that he was proud and conceited, and he **resolved** to trap him; moreover, he felt lonely. He was by no means a good bird; he was constantly managing to get into scrapes; and all the obedient little birds round about shunned him, and would not be **seen** in his company. So he made a low bow, and remarked, in reply, "What a shame, to leave such a fine handsome looking young fellow as you to take care of the young ones, when hundreds, and hundreds of birds of quality would be delighted to make your acquaintance."

Didn't Master Bobby look important now? His red breast heaved with gratified vanity.

Flattery is food for fools; and Ruby had got the advantage at once; so he went on pouring into the

simpleton's ear the most extravagant speeches, and
bare-faced compliments, determined to make him a
greater fool than he was already.

As to Bobby, enraptured **at** having found so discrim-
inating **a** comrade, he hopped about at his side—
and who so fine as he ?—while, in glowing colours, and
over-drawn words, he described the charms and beauties of the country he came from. The delicious **grubs !**
never were there such grubs !   The refreshing brooks !
never were there such brooks !

Farther and farther they flew. Bobby's delight grew
stronger every moment ; and when his new friend
added to **the** other glowing statement, that " he may
do just as he liked, go to rest when he liked, or **not**
go at all,"—he made up his mind to fly away the first
opportunity.

Seeing his advantage, Ruby exclaimed in a joyous
tone, " O, mine is a rare jolly life, **free** as the air
and **wind !** Why don't you come and pay us a visit ?
All my friends will be delighted to show you every
attention."

At first Bobby was startled at the thought of his

open disobedience to his good mother; but Ruby replied, in answer to this objection, that "his mother **need** know nothing about it; he would be home long before she would. Besides," added the crafty tempter, "what a shame, that a fine, brave, handsome fellow like you should be kept in leading strings by your 'mammy,'—taking care of the young ones like a nursery bird."

This was too much for Bobby. The idea of being sneered at! Beside, "What harm can be done by it?" he argued in his own mind. "I can get back long before father and mother come home, and they wont know anything about it."

The point was lost. The tempter had prevailed. Bobby consented to go, and he hopped on by the side of Ruby; now picking up a choice worm, then flying a bit, singing and twittering; in fact, "doing just as they liked," and quite forgetting how quickly the time was stealing away, and how far they had wandered from the beautiful garden.

By and bye Bobby felt tired. His legs ached terribly, and he wished to return; so he gently hinted to his

friend his intention. " O, don't turn back just yet,"
replied Ruby, " we are just close to my father's house."
This was a falsehood, for his real home was far away
yet ; he **had** flown miles from the old spot ; aye, and
sad to relate, he could not find it again.

Somewhat re-assured by his friend's plausible manner, Bobby went on a little further.   They had by this
time left the green fields, and were in th**e dusty** road,
close by the stream, where stood the tumble-down cottage—that very stream, where a few weeks ago his
father first saw his tender, watchful mother.   The two
little disobedient birds stopped to drink some of the
clear bright water that went singing past, shook their
dusty feathers, chased a few long-legged gnats, and
thereby going still farther from home.

Unheeding the lapse of time, the shades of evening
began to draw on ; and as they now hopped and flew
less bravely than they did when they set out, sundry
misgivings took possession of their minds.   Bobby
heaved a deep sigh, and Ruby was not quite so boast-
ful about his grand friends. Presently they heard a
dreadful noise, such a noise as never any disobedient

robins heard in their lives. Then a bright, awful light shone for an instant round, and almost blinded them! Oh, how affrighted they were! They hopped, and flew as fast as fear would let them, till they reached the friendly shade of some fine flag leaves. They were wet and miserable! while louder and louder, nearer and nearer, came the horrible noise, and more blinding became the blue forked lightning! Trembling and downcast, all their fine speeches and boasting forgotten, the unhappy little wanderers dared not move! They expected every moment to be crushed to pieces. What were they **to** do?

The rain fell in wild torrents; the drenched flag leaves flapped heavily over them; their feathers were dripping; they shivered with cold. If they attempted to fly, the pouring rain would beat them into **the earth.**

"Oh, why, why did you tempt me to leave my little brother and sisters, and to disobey my kind good mother?"—exclaimed Bobby, in a distressed tone. "You pleased yourself, and needn't have done it, if you had not liked," retorted Ruby. "No, I didn't; you made me go by your fine descriptions, and telling

F

me how glad your friends would be to see me. I don't
believe you have got any friends ; and if you have, I
don't believe they care a rush about you !" replied
Bobby, in an angry tone ; for conscience lashed him,
and he was glad to throw the blame on any one, to
lighten the load he felt. "You are a fine fellow in
your own eyes, but you are a long way from home,"
sneered Ruby, bitterly !

Bobby couldn't stand this ; he flew at his "dear
friend," and pecked him in the eye till it bled. Ruby
was not a coward, and flew at Bobby's tail, and pecked
out nearly all the feathers he was so proud of. Bobby
retaliated, and one of the fiercest single beaked battles
took place between these two wicked little birds, that
can be found in the annals of redbreast history.

I cannot say I am glad to record that Bobby had
the best of the battle, for he killed his "dear friend,"
by pecking a hole in his head, quite into the brain.

Poor little Ruby ! See what disobedience comes to !
You will readily imagine that Bobby had no enjoyment
in his victory ; quite the contrary. When he saw
Ruby fall down, with his bright eyes all glazed and

bloody, and when, after a terrible quivering, his beautiful little form lay **stiff** and cold, he would have given all the world, if it had been his own, to bring him back again to life. He hopped round and round the tiny corpse, **and** chirped so mournfully, that it would have made you weep to have seen him. Then, tired and sorrow-stricken, he went as **far as he** could from the scene of their battle, and sat moping and desolate, till night drew her dark curtain.

Oh ! what a host of memories rise up before him ! He thought of his gentle, loving mother, and his disobedience to her wise commands ; he thought of noble, unselfish Whistle, and all his own ill-treatment of him : he thought of the many sly pecks and kicks he had given poor delicate Weeney, who bore it all so patiently. " Oh ! that I could but see you **all again, to** tell you how sorry **I am**, and ask you to forgive me ; I would never be **unkind** to you again !"—sobbed the miserable, prodigal bird. But alas ! it was too late ! He had brought all this trouble upon himself, and had no one **to** blame. Longing for his own quiet nest, and the brooding of his mother's warm breast, he crept, as

well as his weary, cold limbs would let him, towards
the old cottage, hoping to make a bed under the dry
thatch.   This brought him again in view of his dead,
false friend Ruby. He had just reached the threshold,
when a strange loud " hoot-a-hoo! **hoot-a-ho-o**!" made
him stop, and tremble violently. His troubles seemed
never to end.

Nearer and nearer came the fearful noise ; and over
his defenceless head were flapping two large wings,
while two eyes were looking down—Oh! such great
eyes!—and a beak—Oh! such **a** crooked beak!—
seemed to point at him! Flap went the wings ; open
went the beak ; and poor Bobby felt his doom was
sealed! **But to** die there all alone ; to feel certain
that he should be eaten up by the young owlets, who
were peeping out of the decayed bark of the old oak
tree! " What shall **I** do? Oh! what will become of
me?" cried Bobby in despair; " where can I hide from
that monster? Ah me! foolish, sinful, miserable bird
that **I am,** I have deserved all this grief and fear, by
my disobedience to the best of mothers."

For a moment or **two** there was **a** pause of dreadful
suspense. Then came the flap! flap! flap! **Nearer**

and nearer it came! The ghastly **face** of the white owl peered **down** close **to that** of poor Bobby. Fear struck **him to the ground.** He gave one **or two faint gasps,** then a short **struggle,** and **he turned on** his **back and** died. You see, in the picture, the great **white owl** carrying poor little Bobby's warm body **to her young ones** —and they will eat him up, and no doubt say what a delicious mouthful **he was. And there** lies Ruby! Whether the great white owl returned again **for** *him* also, I cannot tell; although I should think it most probable he did. If she saw him, as I suppose was the case, she would be quite unwilling to allow **so** delicate a tit-bit to remain near her nest, uneaten **by** her hungry little children.

Poor Bobby! Poor Ruby! **I am truly sorry for** you; but you chose your own ways, and **despised all** the advice of those who knew better than yourselves; and what could you expect? **Farewell,** poor disobe**dient** birds, farewell! I am grieved **for** you, and **so** are my dear young readers, I know; and if they take warning by your fate, you will not have lived and died in vain. Poor Bobby!—poor Ruby!

"The **way of transgressors is hard.**"

CHAPTER V.

" I saw a beggar in the street, and another beggar pitied **him**;
sympathy sank into his soul, and the pitied one felt happier."

SUPPOSE we now take **a peep at the** generous brother
and sisters of silly Bobby. We left them, you recollect, with their beaks under their wings, enjoying a
delicious repose, fatigued with pleasure, and dreaming
away the bright hours. On awakening, they stood up
and stretched themselves, looking anxiously round for
their parents. As they did not **come**, Whistle amused
himself **with one** of his lovely songs, between the notes
of which Chirp thought she heard a feeble cry. Looking round, she exclamed, " Hark, brother! do hark!
I am sure I heard a **cry** of pain."

Vexed **at** being interrupted, just **as he** was resting
on a note he had been some time trying to reach,
Whistle replied, rather hastily, "Well, well, Weeney
dear, what if it is? It's nothing to **us**." But gentle
Weeney would not be put off; she would not let him

rest; **so,** putting her little head close to his, she replied, "Oh, dear brother, suppose that sorrowful note **should** be our poor Bobby; do, *do* go, and see!"

To oblige **Weeney,** of whom he was very **fond,** Whistle left off singing, and listened. A very plaintive note was borne towards them by the soft breeze. Whistle became interested. "I'll just pop out and see," he remarked. "**Oh** no! don't get out of that sheltered bush, dear brother," exclaimed Chirp; "you know mother told us not to stir till she came back. Let us call to the poor bird, and ask if we can do anything for it." Again the cry seemed to come nearer. "O, its only a poor plain brown sparrow," said Whistle. "Only a poor sparrow! Oh, brother! even a **sparrow** can feel pain; do call it; perhaps we can **do something** to help it," persisted Weeney.

Now, I think Master Whistle must have "got out of bed on **the** wrong **side**" that morning, as people say, for certainly he was in a mood very unusual with him, as he was **a** sweet-tempered, obliging bird generally. So he answered, "I am not going to make myself hoarse, shrieking after a sparrow, I promise you." **And let** me add, I think he was a little vexed at having his song interrupted; for you have heard that he was somewhat proud of his voice, and vanity invariably leads to other sins.

Chirp did not like to look upon Weeney's sad eyes; so she called as loudly as she could, "What is **the** matter, Master Brown Coat? Pray **come,** and take shelter in our comfortable bush." In a few moments, limping along, and dragging after him one of his legs, came Master Brown Coat. "Oh!" exclaimed Weeney, "look, brother, look at his poor leg! it is bleeding: **who can** have been so cruel as to hurt the poor little thing?" "Come close to us, we will warm you," exclaimed Chirp; and the two loving sisters made room for the fainting bird between them. "Are you hungry?" softly inquired Weeney; and then added, quickly, "our eldest brother will be home soon, **and** he will go and find you some nice food."

"*I* will go, *I* will go," said generous, repentant Whistle; and was in the act of hopping down, when the stranger bird stopped him, by saying, in a low **voice,** "I am not hungry, kind friends; I am too

ill to eat; and believe I am dying; but I could not
without thanking you, from my heart, for your kind
and generous conduct towards a poor stranger; by
warning you with my last breath, never to disobey
the commands of your dear father and mother, and
leaving your nests or your snug hiding-places. If
you do, either unfeeling boys, or men with dreadful
things full of noise **and fire**, will destroy you; or
you may stray into a trap, set for you by thoughtless,
cruel children. Many a time, as I sat beside my dear
mother on the house-top, watching these proceedings,
has she said to me—and my mother was a knowing
bird—" My child, it often happens that people who set
traps for others fall into traps themselves;" and **I**
found her words true; for the cruel boy who let **off one**
of those things full of fire and noise, and covered with
rust, which gave me my death wound, blew off one of
his own fingers, and he will be a cripple in his hand
for ever." As he uttered this warning, his little voice
gradual**ly** grew fainter. Once more he feebly thanked
the three kind birds for their compassion towards a
stranger, and then, after a short struggle and a
mournful chirp, **he died.**

Every one of the kind birds fell to sobbing, as they saw poor Brown Coat breathe his last; and Whistle, ashamed of his tears, yet unable to hide them, exclaimed, as he brushed them away with his wing, " I should like to catch that **cruel** boy that killed poor Brown Coat. I'd peck out both his eyes!" "Oh! brother, dear," replied Weeney, "don't **say** such shocking things as those. I'm sure you wouldn't **do any** such thing; you would be sorry that he was so naughty and cruel, and hope he will live and learn to do better, and be kind and thoughtful for others. Besides, I don't **think** it is so much the fault of the boys themselves, as it is of their parents, who allow them to carry those fearful guns. What do you say, Chirp?"

" I agree with you, dearest Weeney," answered her sister, " and I think there ought to be a law made, to prevent boys from using ' fire arms;' **how** should they know the proper use of them, indeed? I hope," added Chirp, " it will be a lesson to the foolish boy who lost his finger, not to play with guns again."

Thus conversing, the time passed away; and I am glad to record my sincere approval of the conduct of these young sisters, not only in their compassion towards poor wounded Brown Coat, but in giving Master Whistle a lesson, not to despise a neighbour, because he is poorly and meanly clad. Many a warm heart beats under a shabby coat; and many a mean spirit dwells under silks, and satins, and showy accomplishments. And remember, dear **children, that**

> " Whene'er **we lend** to others **aid,**
> We always shall be well repaid."

Not that we should do good with the idea of being repaid—that would be selfish—but because doing good naturally results in reward to those who do it.

A few moments after the above sad occurrence, the clouds began to lower, and the sky became overcast. Seeing that a storm was brewing, Mr. and Mrs. Robin took a hasty leave of their friends, returned to their children, and placed them in safety, completely sheltered by the wall and **the** friendly ivy.

But Bobby—where was Bobby? His brother and sisters could give their anxious parents no information respecting him. They chirped! and chirped! and chirped! but still no answer came. Mrs. Robin wished to go in search of him, but her careful husband persuaded her not **to** risk her life for one who had acted so contrary to his parents' wishes. She pleaded very hard, **but** just then **a vivid** flash of lightning, and a loud thunder clap, decided **the question.** The fond mother found enough to do to comfort those who were left. Weeney became quite ill, and shook, and trembled, and trembled again, till her legs refused to **support her; and** had not her father's strong wing held her up, she would have fallen down and died.

When the storm was over, they related poor Brown Coat's melancholy end, and the advice he had given them with his dying breath. Very much gratified were their parents to know that their precepts had not been disregarded, but that their offspring **had** shown so much kindness towards the forlorn stranger. Even Whistle had acknowledged his fault, and told his mother he "was so sorry" **he** had spoken harshly, and said he would " never do so again."

Day after day they all watched, and watched, but no sight of Bobby! O, how they all looked out for his

return; but alas! he never came again; and long did
hope linger in his poor mother's breast, after it had
died out of the hearts of all beside. About a fortnight
or three weeks after the storm, Whistle, being grown a
fine strong bird, they resolved to remove to a short
distance; but Weeney, poor little Weeney, was a sad
trial to them all. Instead of growing stronger, as she
grew older, she became day by day weaker; and her
parents feared she would never be strong enough to
provide her own living, and take care of herself. Truly
it was a great trial to them; but the love of parents to
their little ones, and always to the weakest and crip-
pled ones—if such there be—is a wonderful and lovely
thing. Dear children! never vex your kind father, or
bring tears into the eyes of your tender mother. If
you do, the memory of your sin will be a heavy load,
when they are sleeping in the old churchyard.

Then, as to Weeney Robin, though her slender legs
often ached, and her appetite failed daily, she was both
cheerful and contented. No murmuring, no impatience,
no envy, ever disturbed her gentle bosom. She would
take the bitter herb her mother brought her as medi-

cine—in the hope it would cure her, and make her
strong—without one word of complaint. Weeney never
made a fuss, or set up a cry, or shook her head, and
spat the medicine out of her mouth, as I have seen
children do. I hope **none** of my little readers' consciences accuse them in **this** respect. Mary, Fanny,
Bessie, Freddy, Johnny, what say **you**? Have you
ever disturbed the whole house, because **you had a**
powder or pill to take, to do you good? **If** you have
done so, for shame! Pray resolve never to be such a
baby again. Think of good Weeney, and don't be
outdone by a bird.

As **you** may easily imagine, these gentle, patient
ways endeared the delicate bird very much **to** all her
family and friends. Every one would do what they
could for " poor dear Weeney." As to Whistle, he
made such a pet of her! never was the like! There
was nothing he would not give up to her, even his
dearly loved notes, of the sound of which he was so
proud, if it made her head ache. Poor little Weeney!
Whenever she dies she will be as much missed and
lamented as any bird in the country.

At an early hour on the following morning, Mr.
Robin shook his plumage, feathered himself, and
washed his beak in a tuft hard by. Whistle did the
same. He had always been taught to be a clean and
tidy bird; never to leave his night's shelter without
attending to his plumage. His parents had earnestly
impressed on all their brood the great importance of
cleanliness. "No **matter," they would** say, "if you
cannot make your feathers so smooth at your first
attempt, *try again.* Go on; never give up. 'Slow
and steady wins the race'—and 'whatever is worth
doing **at all** is worth doing well.'"

With all such good advice as this constantly before
them, we may be sure the young birds learnt to **do**
everything in a proper manner; and seldom slovened
over their morning's washings, or **neglected** their personal appearance. This strict attention to neatness
and order was sometimes neglected by Miss Chirp,
who, though kind and good generally, had certainly
this failing—and a difficult one she found it to over-
come—the love of ease, and of putting off a disagreeable duty until a more convenient time should arrive—

which *convenient* time never *did* arrive, and never *will* arrive.

Poor Chirp was oftentimes very sorry for her neglect, and used to promise her good mother to do better in future; but, like many little girls that I know, she forgot, in a few weeks, her promise of amendment; and thus again fell under punishment. **Hence, you will** quite understand how particular Whistle was, never to presume to accompany his father, unless he was neat and clean.

Before they parted from Mrs. Robin, and the young lady birds, they all joined in their morning hymn of praise—a custom they never neglected. Then Mr. Robin, and Whistle took their flight, passing over many wide fields and beautiful hedges, clustering with roses and honeysuckles. Then they stopped **on** a common, covered with gorse and heather, quite dazzling to the unexperienced eyes of Whistle. First, he stopped to admire the bright yellow gorse; and, forgetting to ask his father's permission, he hopped upon a bush covered with scented flowers; and, oh! what a sharp prick he got!

How soon he repented his rashness! Hearing him chirp piteously, his father looked **up**. There was son Whistle, struggling, and sinking deeper and deeper amidst the sharp prickles.

"Why, Whistle, my boy!" exclaimed Robin, "**how** came you there? You are in a sad predicament!"

"Oh! father dear, the bush looked so beautiful!" pleaded poor Whistle.

"And like all **young birds,** you were caught by the outside show; but recollect, 'all is not gold that glitters,'" replied Robin: and **then** added, in a cheerful tone, "however, make a brave effort, my boy; **a** long pull, and a strong pull, and you will **soon** be **out.** Now give one good jump, and it will be all right."

Whistle did as his father directed him; and, penitent and crest-fallen, he **will** remember **in** future not to be too hasty in forming an opinion about appearances.

As they hopped along, Mr. Robin remarked to his son, "Always recollect that heather is a safe plant; many a time **I** have sheltered **under its** purple blossoms."

G

" What makes the grass and heath so short in some places?" asked Whistle.

" We are coming to the more retired spots, my dear son," replied Robin, " where the little brown rabbit loves to dwell ; and they feed upon the heath, and nibble the blue harebell, and the scented thyme ; **and they** **burrow** under the earth, deep **down in their warm** nests, in those little holes."

" How dark it must be all down under ground ; I should **not** like to live where it is always night," suggested Whistle.

Robin looked puzzled. He scratched his head with his little toe, and an idea seemed to strike him— " Why, you see, my son, they are rabbits, and we are birds ; therefore birds cannot do as rabbits do, nor can rabbits do as birds do. We love the fresh, pure air, and the tops of trees, and the habitation of man. They do not. They are afraid of man, and **run** away from him ; while we love his resorts, and return his little kindnesses to us with our best song. Altogether, we have **not much** to complain of. When the snow covers the ground, and the **bright** holly berries hang on the

trees; when food is scarce, and many of our fellow-
birds die with hunger, how often do dear little children
save the crumbs, and save us dainty meals! How often
we hop on the window sills, and find them strewed with
tit bits! Kind little benefactors! to put your small
white hands out in the cold to feed us poor robins!
And recollect, my son, that we, little birds, must be
faithful. We must cheer them with our sweetest song.
We must be their humble Christmas friends. By all,
and every one, we must be called their ' little winter
friends, dear Robin Redbreasts!' Now think of these
things when you are alone in the world, son Whistle."

Son Whistle bowed his head, and his father's words
evidently made a deep impression on him.

For several days in succession the two birds flew
over the neighbouring fields, and lanes, and commons;
and, as you may easily imagine, my dear young friends,
" Son Whistle" gained a good deal of experience and
knowledge from Mr. Robin's sage counsels and advice.
He was now able to fly about alone; and, unlike poor
wilful Bobby, he would not listen to any bird that
wanted to entice him away, or to get him into mis-

chief; but the very moment he saw his danger, he would stretch his strong young wings, and fly away; never even stopping **to** look either to the right or left, till he perched on the twig at his old garden home. Over hedges and ditches, fields and cottages, common and lane, on he went, straight as the old crow flies.

One afternoon our bird friend had **been** away beyond his usual time in search of the most delicate insects **for** his invalid sister. This was one of his favourite occupations; for he dearly loved Weeney.

On his return, he was startled to see a little group **of** friends assembled round their mid-day resting place. His dear father and mother stood with their heads bowed down on their breasts with grief; their tails drooped gloomily to the earth, and it was evident no common sorrow was busy at their hearts.

Poor Chirp wept, and would not **be** pacified. The thrush, **in** the laurel above their heads, chanted forth a **mournful** song. The goldfinch hushed his low soft notes; and little Jenny Wren—the

" Little Jenny Wren, **that** was sick upon a time,
    And little Robin Redbreast brought her cake and wine,"

of which no doubt you have heard—lifted up her *wee*
head out of the cozy hole in the ivy by their side, gave
three plaintive chirps, and, in soft tones, begged them
to be comforted ; whilst a grey-headed sparrow sobbed
aloud, as he remembered the kindness, once shown to
his poor wounded son by her—the loving-hearted, gentle Weeney—who had, a few minutes before, bid adieu
for ever to the green fields, and blue skies, and glad
sunshine of this beautiful world.

Long **they** mourned their loss over the little lifeless
form of **her** they all so truly loved.

Suddenly, their grief was broken by the sound of
youthful feet on the gravel walk, and laughing voices
in the clear air ; and soon the curly heads and rosy
faces of the rectory children came in sight, **as in** high
glee, they chased some magnificent gold and purple
butterflies over the lawn, through the rose bushes,
down the gravel walks, here, there, and everywhere.

By **and** bye, little Emmeline espied the desolate
group of birds ; and, **child** like, peeped inquisitively to
see what they were all about.

The Robins knew the dear girl **would not harm**

them ; they therefore only hopped away a step or two ;
but this movement was sufficient to reveal to the kind-
hearted child the stiff, lifeless body of Weeney.

Tenderly taking up the dead bird, she laid it in
her white pinafore, and called to a fine looking little
black-haired lad, at the other end of the lawn, " Come,
brother, come ! Here's a poor little dead robin in my
pinafore. I picked it up from under the bushes.
Make haste and see it ; how still it lies, with its bright
eyes shut !"

Bounding towards her came the brother called, and
behind him Helena ; whilst Alfred and Fred brought
up the rear. Gently were the soft feathers smoothed
down by their young fingers, as they looked on the
motionless robin.

" Poor little thing ! poor little thing !" they said,
tenderly, and in sorrowful tones. Emmeline suggested, " Shall we dig the darling a little grave in our
own garden by the arbour, and bury the poor little
robin ?"

" Yes ! oh yes ! that we will !" exclaimed the children at once. " I've got some pasteboard, that will
just do for a nice little box," eagerly chimed in Helena.

Then, at brother Herbert's suggestion, they adjourned to the summer house, and deposited the dead bird in one corner, covered over with Fred's cap, while the little girls went for the implements of labour. Then they returned with the much prized pasteboard, needle, thread, and thimble. Alfred added a nice piece of wool, to lay at the bottom of the box, to make it "soft and comfortable," as he told them.

Oh! how busy they were all in a minute! and how fast their tongues ran! How soon the small, odd looking box was stitched together! How gently they laid Weeney in her warm bed, and then placed it on a long piece of wood, which said piece of wood performed many and various duties—sometimes it was converted into a seat, (and a very uneasy one I used to think it)—sometimes thrown over some stones that were piled up close by, as a see-saw—sometimes one thing, sometimes another. In the present instance, this most accommodating piece of wood, as I before observed, was turned into a litter; and in the centre of which was placed the small cardboard box, containing the dead body of little Weeney.

How demurely the four children each held a corner
of this new-fashioned conveyance, as they walked along
the gravel path, until they regained their best garden
plot, and deposited the poor bird in its quiet resting-place in the hole dug by brother Herbert! There,
overshadowed by the drooping flowers of the graceful
laburnum, and perfumed by the odour of the white and
purple lilac blossoms, sleeps gentle, loving Weeney!

While the boys were filling up the tiny grave, they
observed some robins at a distance, watching their proceedings very attentively; and for many a day after-
wards, when the children were digging near the spot,
a little robin would be hopping constantly about, growing so tame that he would **even** perch on Herbert's
spade, and pick **up** the worms and grubs, as he turned
them up from the newly dug earth.

To the present day, strange to relate, it is a favourite
resort of the redbreasts. They sit about poor Weeney's
grave, as if they knew it was her last resting-place;
and who knows but that they are telling their young
nestlings of her gentle and obedient character—of her
loving nature, and of her early death? Who can tell

that **they** are not holding her up as an example of kindness and imitation, for the time to come, to all **little** birds; so **that** when they depart this life they may **be held up to** admiration? What **a** delightful thing **it is to** be so sweet and amiable, that all **your** friends love you while you live, and weep over your memory long after you have passed **away!**

My dear little readers, Weeney **was** only **a** bird. When her small **body was put into** the box, out of sight **in the** earth, there **was** an end of her. But when *you* are called away, though **the same** earth may **cover you** up, there will not be an end of *you*. There **is a great** difference between a little child and **a little** bird. Ah! **a** very great difference! *You* have a never-dying soul, which will be for ever blest, or for ever miserable. Just **think** what a solemn thought this is— "I must live for **ever in** joy or woe! **I have a soul** that never dies!"

Dear child, would you **wish to** live **for ever** in woe? Ah no! no! no! Then **go** to the **child's** loving Friend. **Go to Jesus** to save you. He *will* **do so.** He died to save *you*—to save every little boy and girl from sin, **from sorrow, and from death.**

See the kind Shepherd, Jesus, stands
   With all-engaging charms ;
Hark ! how he **calls** the tender lambs,
   And folds them in his arms.

The feeblest lamb amidst the flock
   Shall be its Shepherd's care ;
While, folded **in** the Saviour's **arms,**
They're safe from every snare.

CHAPTER VI.

NOTHING of importance occurred to our Robins after Weeney's early death. Their two remaining children, Chirp and Whistle, profited by the advice of their dear parents, and tried to follow in their footsteps.

The latter, as he grew older, saw the folly and foolishness of thinking so highly of himself, and of setting so much value on his fine voice; so he became a modest, retiring, well-informed bird, using his musical notes, not for his own gratification, but for the pleasure of others; hence, "Young Whistle Robin" was always considered a great attraction at all the little morning and evening concerts given by the surrounding birds.

At the rectory he was a "dear, darling redbreast;" and many a village child would stop, on her way to school, to listen to his song, and admire his fine plumage.

In the spring following the death of Weeney, he took unto himself a mate,—such a sweet little thing!—

and when they built their nest, they still clung to the
favourite old spot, and loved the beautiful garden, and
pleasant old church ; and they taught their little ones
to be good and happy, to love each other, and be dutiful, obedient birds.

. So attached, indeed, is " Mr. Whistle" to the village
where so many days of his happy bird-childhood were
passed, that he has taught his children to love all con-
nected with it. In fact, I don't believe the race of
Redbreasts will ever be extinct in the neighbourhood.

I have not said very much of Miss Chirp, except
that she " tried" to be very kind-hearted ; always
anxious to do good to the little birds around her ; help-
ing the weak, giving a kind chirp to those in trouble ;
but, especially, using her best and sweetest note, in
teaching those of her young feathered friends, who had
lost their parents, or were unmindful of their offspring,
the comfort and importance of singing their earliest
song to that great and glorious God who made them,
and placed them in this beautiful world, amid flowers
and shrubs of every kind ; warming them with the
bright beams of His sun, as it rides through the

heavens; lighting them at night with the mild rays of His silvery moon; sheltering them by night and by day, with the thick and leafy foliage of trees and hedges, mossy banks, reeds, and rushes; and quenching their thirst in the little running rills, meandering streams, and silent pools.

My dear children, do you remember, every morning, this kind, this bountiful Creator? Do you lift up your hearts in love **to** him? Do you give Him your first, early song of prayer and praise? And do you remem**ber** Him, when the gentle curtain of night is folded around the earth, ere you lay down your little heads to rest on your warm pillows? Do you remember to thank Him for his care, and goodness, **and pro**tection through the past day? If you have ever forgotten this song of love and praise, pray **that** you may not forget it in future; seek to be guided aright, so that the words of your mouth may be acceptable to God; praising Him for " His goodness, His wonderful works to the children of men."

To return to Miss Chirp Robin. It is a good thing to try, aye, a good thing to try *again*, **and AGAIN.** It is

a good thing to be kind hearted : it is a blessed thing.
All little children should ever recollect this ; and strive
and pray to become like Him, who was "meek and
lowly in heart," and *very* tender to the lambs of His
fold.   And Miss Chirp was quite right in wishing and
striving to do good, and to help others.   But Miss
Chirp had failings ; she was not always good ; she had
to *try* again, and *again*.

I am always sorry to record the faults and miscon-
duct of others ; in this instance, that is, in again
reverting to Chirp, I only speak of her's by way of
warning to any dear girl who may read this story.
Miss Chirp Redbreast was—I blush to record the
fact—inclined to be very slovenly and untidy.   For
example—after her dear parents would have left the
nest, or the sheltering ivy, neat as a new pin, she
would feather herself, and allow the down and dust to
fly all about their clean resting-place ; just as I have
seen little girls leave their combs and brushes out of
place, and laying about.   Then she would drop the
food off her beak, and never think to wipe it away.

Now, really, I do say, if there is one thing more

unpleasant than another, it is to see young people—
aye, and grown up people too, for that matter—slovenly
at meals. Depend upon it, whenever you find this the
case, they are negligent in everything else. Untidy
heads of hair—untidy frocks and pinafores—untidy
shoes—untidy stockings about their heels—untidy
everything!

I knew a little girl—who is now growing a great
girl—who, I grieve to say, from not striving against
this habit of slovenliness, never knows where to put
her hand upon a thing in her possession. She can
never find her thimble or her needle—and if, perchance,
she does find them, sure as sure can be, she cannot
find her cotton, or scissors; and frequently I have
seen her wasting precious hours hunting for her goods
and chattels—hours, which might have been employed
so much better! "A place for every thing, and every
thing in its place," is an excellent maxim.

I sometimes think that if a prize had been given at
the Great Exhibition to the writer of children's books,
who "leaves off about the story, to tell something else,"
I should have obtained that prize. Somehow, I cannot

help running off the course, like self-willed ponies do at times.

I cannot refrain bringing into my tale, **little,** old-fashioned, **odd** pieces of memory; and now, even at the risk of being called a " tiresome old thing " by some Master Jack, or Miss Lucy, I *must* just tell an anecdote of a little girl, that comes—and I **am** sure I never **invited** it—pop! into my mind. For convenience **sake** I shall call her Laura, but remember that was **not her** real name.

"Laura, my love, do not forget to run on the little piece of braid you tore off your frock when you were trying it **on,**" exclaims the watchful mother to Miss Laura.

" Never fear, mamma **dear; I** will be sure to do **it** before I dress for the evening," replied the young lady, tripping gaily into the drawing-room **with** what seemed like a basket of flowers, **to** decorate the vases, etc.

"Have you done that little piece of work yet, darling?" again demands mamma, a few hours later.

"No, mamma, but I shall be sure not to forget it," answered the busy maiden ; and of course she did not

mean to " forget it,"—but a disastrous habit of " doing
it by and bye," when it ought to **be** done *at once*, did
all the mischief.

The clock strikes nine! All within the house is
light, and joy, and gladness. Carriages rattle up **to**
the door, and deposit cargoes of life and beauty, to
rattle away again to make room for others.

O dear! I quite forgot to tell you there is to be a
grand party to-night. **It** is the birthday of Laura's
eldest brother, **and** " fine doings " are " going on,"—as
the villagers declare one to another.

I should just like to let you all peep " inside.'
What grand old pictures, in grand old frames! What
glittering ornaments, scattered about! What inspirit-
ing strains of music, and what heaps, and heaps of
flowers ; dear, darling, precious flowers ! Then, too—
what greetings, among the " young ladies !" and what
shaking of hands, and bowings, and scrapings, among
the " young gentlemen !" " Who but they?" as the
page remarks to Anne, the under nursemaid !

Ah! there are sweet young faces there ; fair, young
forms, and, no doubt, loving hearts! I love to think so.

H

Well, all goes on "merry as a wedding bell" for
a while; but by and bye, in the very middle of a game
of forfeits, there is a loud noise, something between a
tumble, a scramble, and a scream, outside in the hall!

In less than a second, troops of youngsters gather
round the cause of the alarm—no less a personage
than Miss Laura herself—who has caught her foot in
the wandering braid, and tumbled down stairs; provi-
dentially, with no other injury to herself, than that of
knocking out one of her beautiful front teeth against
the corner of the rail, on which she came down plump.
I was going to say, " serves her right,"—but that is a
hard, mean feeling; and really I never liked Laura so
well, in all her "growing up," as I did on that night;
when, suppressing the pain she must have felt, with
noble heroism, she frankly and candidly told all her
young friends the cause of her disaster.

Dear girl! many and many a sermon did that va-
cant place in her pretty mouth preach to her, I can
tell you; and at the present time, there is not a more
primitive, orderly creature in the village of——.

I must not tell the name of the village, or you may

guess **her's** also, and that will never do. I wish to keep it secret ; so **pray do not walk** up to any charming young friend of **your acquaintance, who** has had the misfortune to loss **one** of her front teeth, and whisper, " Pray, **are you** Miss Laura, that tumbled down stairs **on your** brother Peter's birthday, and knocked out your tooth ?"—for, I repeat, Laura **was not her** *real* name.

My dear little girl, **are you tidy ?** It is a plain question ; but I am a **plain person, and I love** little people dearly, **and dislike to see** them slovens, and that is the real **truth.** Now if conscience whispers, " You know, **Mary, or** Jane, or Louisa, or Anne—you often vex your patient mother by your untidiness, and disobey her wishes, **when** she is anxious to make **you a neat,** tidy child ?" Pray resolve from this moment to give up all your careless habits, and be henceforth as neat and nice, as " a new dolly out of a band-box."

In coming back to Miss Chirp Redbreast, I repeat I am **sorry** to speak **of her** failings : but there is no such thing as perfection, whether in birds or children. The best of birds is but a bird at best. As it may give you a hint, my reader, I will **just** briefly tell you the

wise steps Mrs. Robin Redbreast took to cure her somewhat wilful daughter.

Of course, after the usual friendly calls had been
made with all the neighbouring families, an exchange
of those civilities **took** place ; and there was **a very**
well-informed, well-behaved brood, the offspring **of**
Roseate Redbreast, Esq., **with** which Chirp was anxious
to be acquainted ; indeed they were **looked upon as**
some of the best people in the trees and hedges.

Well, one morning Chirp had been unusually lazy
and untidy. She had never feathered herself, nor
wiped her beak ; in short, she had **not** properly dressed
after breakfast, nor before, though she had sundry commands to " **go and** make herself neat." As she paid
no attention to her mother's wishes, but seemed drowsy
and idle, she was very wisely sent out **of** the nest,
with strict orders " not to return until **she had obeyed**
the commands of her parent." Chirp very reluctantly
obeyed. She had half a mind to be pert ; and I believe her mother had to speak twice before she moved.

Now just mark how disobedience ever brings its own
punishment. As soon as Miss Chirp got outside the

nest, she took wing, and flew about twenty yards away, and perched on the twig of a cherry tree in the rectory garden, taking care, however, to keep the nest in sight, —and then she went off to sleep.

About half-an-hour after her departure, who should make their appearance but Mr. and the Misses Roseate Redbreast? After the usual kind enquiries respecting the health of their families, Mrs. Roseate Redbreast asked for Miss Chirp, and spoke of her graceful form, and gentle, kind manners. Mrs. Robin told them the truth, that she was " not at home"—but, like a good mother as she was, she never told them *why*—hoping the lesson and the disappointment would do her daughter more good than exposing her faults to these young favourites, who evidently were pleased to be the acquaintances of a family so intimate at the rectory, and other places of distinction.

After a little while these friends took their departure, begging Mrs. Robin Redbreast to bring Miss Chirp very soon to spend a long evening with them, while Mrs. Roseate looked back, and said, " We shall be happy to see Mr. Whistle also ; we admire his voice exceedingly, and Mr. Roseate thinks him amongst the most agreeable birds of the country."

Poor Chirp! Fancy her annoyance when she learnt that the young ladies she had so long sighed to meet had been at the nest! She came to grief, indeed, especially when she heard " they are such nice, well-behaved birds." However, it was a lesson to her, I promise you. From that time forth she resolved to try more heartily to conquer her bad habit, and I am glad to tell you she succeeded ; as all may succeed who say, relying on God's help, " It shall be done."

I think that perhaps the death of poor Weeney had a solemn, softening effect on Chirp, and helped to make her more watchful and obedient. She felt her loss deeply, and resolved to become a comfort to her mother, now that her sister was no more. So she grew up a lovely lady bird, and remained with her parents at the old home during the following winter.

When the snow flakes fell, and " the old woman was plucking her geese," as children say, and covering the earth with a spotless robe, Chirp would wing her way to the little scarlet holly tree, and sing her most cheerful song—quite certain that she would be well provided for by the little people at the old nursery window. Then, when the little stars came out, " twinkling one by one,"

> " Up above the world so high,
> Like a diamond in the sky—"

and when the moon **rose** higher **and** higher **on** her silvery track, Chirp would think of **her** happy nest in the dear quiet old church, and shelter herself in the thick ivy opposite her favourites' window.

She seemed to know every one of the rectory **chil-dren**, especially little curly-headed Emmeline, **whose** clear, ringing laugh, and whose sweet little **voice**— " Bobby! Bobby! darling bird! here are plenty of crumbs for your dinner "—filling **her** with delight. Sometimes she would amuse herself **by** peeping through the curtains at the bright fire-light within, listening to the cracking logs of wood, and the blazing fir cones.

Then, after the winter was past, gradually she would watch the light fade away. **The** curfew **from** the church tower would strike, proclaiming that eight

o'clock was come ; and as its echoes died away, she
would creep still further into the ivy, and tucking her
little head under her wing, would betake herself to
rest, with loving thoughts and kindly feelings towards
every one ; and soon her lids closed, and she slept
soundly.

Early in the following spring Chirp left her parental
home, as the happy wife of Mr. Hotspur Redbreast,
the second son of Roseate Redbreast, Esq., of whom
mention has been made. They built themselves one
of the neatest, loveliest nests ever seen ; and in due
time **four** little baby birds gladdened their hearts, and
gave them plenty of employment. I doubt not but
Mrs. Hotspur Redbreast took especial pains to render
her children neat and tidy, remembering her own early
lessons, and that she trained them to be happy, good,
and useful.

Our first friends, Mr. and Mrs. Robin, enjoyed a
good old age, beloved and respected by all who knew
them ; and at last they were buried near the spot
where their darling Weeney rested, and where neither
owl, nor hawk, nor even cream-loving Dora, could get
at them.

Now I doubt not but my little readers are all wishing to know what became of the nest that was built in the desk of the dear old church. Carefully covered over by a glass shade, it stands, at this moment, **in my** drawing-room, one of the most valued treaures there, I assure you. No dust, nor mischievous little fingers are ever allowed to touch it. **It is** far too precious ! And if any of my **young** readers would like to see it, they are quite welcome to come to the rectory, and I will not **only** show that to them, but also the old church, the ancient Bible, and the curious yew branch growing out, so remarkably, from the tower.

And, moreover, if any of you, dear children, on **a** Sabbath morning, should wend your steps towards, and enter the quiet village church, you **will most** probable renew your acquaintance with the once "little Herbert," who dug poor Weeney's grave, but who is now the beloved curate, and helper of the old rector. The once happy boy is now the happy husband, the faithful pastor, the poor's friend !

And now, my dear young friends, ere I conclude, let me ask, for what purpose, think you, have I written this story? Why have I looked back upon bygone years, filled with so many memories, and why have I recalled them? Do you think it was simply to amuse you, or to make the dull hours of a dull day pass less heavily? Not so, dear children. I desire to improve you, to help your good resolutions, and make you glean from history many a useful lesson, many a kindly precept. Do not, then, lay aside the book without a serious thought, and earnest prayer to be made good, obedient, loving children.

Learn, while in the house of prayer and praise, to reverence your gracious and merciful Heavenly Father; and ask Him to help you to become like His dear Son, " who did no sin, neither was guile found in His mouth,"—who loves and cares for all little children, and even for *birds*. Look at the eighty-fourth Psalm, and the third verse, and read what the Book says about it: I think that is a very beautiful verse.

There is another verse I am very fond of, where the blessed Saviour tells the unbelieving people He came to save, that " He would have gathered them as a hen gathers her brood under her wings, but they would not." *Would* not! Oh! what a sad and fearful thought! They WOULD NOT go to Him—the loving—merciful—gracious One—to be saved from everlasting sorrow and suffering!

Did you ever watch the little chickens, frightened, perhaps, at seeing a cruel hawk in the air, or a stealthy cat in the farm yard, how they run chirping and terrified to their anxious mother? And did you ever notice how glad she seemed, when she had them all safe under her warm, sheltering wing?

Then, too, did you ever notice how distressed and agitated she becomes, if one little nestling has wandered beyond the others, and cannot get back to its own safe place? Ah! that is just like the loving Saviour. *He* sees the hawk—that great enemy, " the devil, who goeth about seeking whom he may devour " —among children, as well as among grown-up people ; and the kind Lord of angels stretches forth his hand, and says, " Come unto me ; I will shelter, and save you !"

And again, if one little wanderer strays away, and is led into sin, and finds the way hard and bitter, how anxious He is till it is once more safe in His arms! This reminds me of that most lovely of all written stories, about the "Lost Sheep." You will find it in the fifteenth chapter of St. Luke.

Dear child, will you not be among the little ones who run to the outstretched arms of Jesus? Will you not give Him your heart? Will you not make haste, and "hide yourself in his tender bosom?" Oh! do! No sorrows shall harm you *there*. No "hawk" shall ter-**rify you *there*. No** storms or tempests shall overwhelm you *there*. And even death—that foe alike of all—shall not harm you *there*, for

> "Jesus can make the dying bed
> Softer than downy pillows are."

Dear, **dear** child, come to Jesus, and He **will make** you happy as the days are long.

Farewell! May **we** meet in that bright land, where all is joy, and peace, and love; where, clothed in the **white** robe of **the** Saviour's righteousness, we may shine as the stars for ever and ever!

FAREWELL!

BIRMINGHAM :

WHITE AND PIKE, PRINTERS, COMMERCIAL BUILDINGS